williambee

williambee

Stanley

the Farmer

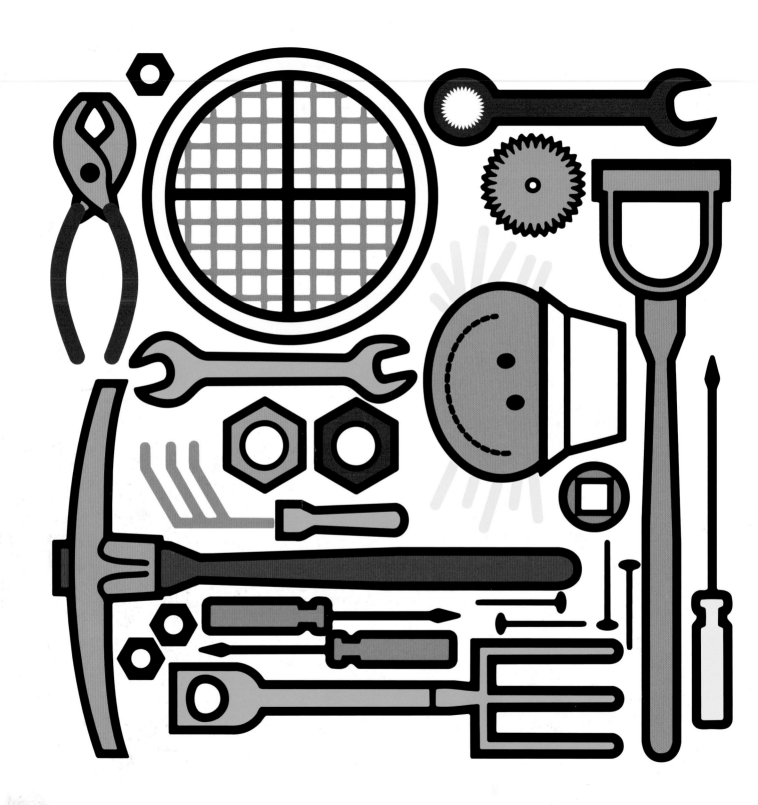

WHEAT
SEEDS

Published by
PEACHTREE PUBLISHERS
1700 Chattahoochee Avenue
Atlanta, Georgia 30318-2112
www.peachtree-online.com

Text and illustrations © 2014 by William Bee

First published in Great Britain in 2014 by Jonathan Cape,
an imprint of Random House Children's Publishers UK
First United States version published in 2015 by Peachtree Publishers

Composition by Melanie McMahon Ives
Illustrations rendered digitally

Printed in October 2014 by Leo Paper Products in China
10 9 8 7 6 5 4 3 2 1 (hardcover)
10 9 8 7 6 5 4 3 2 1 (paperback)
First Edition

Library of Congress Cataloging-in-Publication Data

Bee, William.
Stanley the farmer / by William Bee.
pages cm
ISBN 978-1-56145-803-5 (hardcover) 978-1-56145-859-2 (paperback)
Summary: "It's going to be a busy day down on Stanley's Farm! From plowing the field, to planting the seeds,
to harvesting the wheat, Stanley and his friends Shamus and Little Woo have a lot to do."—Provided by publisher.
[1. Farm life—Fiction. 2. Hamsters—Fiction. 3. Rodents—Ficton.] I. Title.
PZ7.B38197Su 2015
[E]—dc23
2014006502

williambee
Stanley
the Farmer

Ω
PEACHTREE
ATLANTA

Where is Stanley?
He is going to be very busy
today on his farm.

The first thing to do is plow the field
so Stanley can plant some wheat.
He pulls the green plow
with his red tractor.

Shamus helps Stanley
spread manure.

It's smelly work!

Stanley drives the tractor up and down the field while Shamus pours seeds into the hopper.

Now Little Woo is helping too!
They water the seeds twice a day.

The wheat is growing quickly, but Stanley is worried that the birds will eat it.

So he puts up a scarecrow.
Hope it works, Stanley!

Now Stanley's wheat field looks beautiful!

Stanley is very pleased.

Next Stanley needs to cut it all down.
He uses his big green combine.

The grain goes into the sacks,
and the straw comes out of the back.

The blue baler makes the
straw into nice, neat bales.
All finished!

Stanley gives Shamus and Little Woo
a lift back on his trailer.

Thank you, Shamus!
Thank you, Little Woo!

Well! What a busy day!

Stanley's
House

Time for supper!
Time for a bath!

And time for bed!
Goodnight, Stanley.

Stanley

If you liked **Stanley the Farmer** then you'll love these other books about Stanley:

Stanley the Builder
Stanley's Diner
Stanley's Garage

williambee